Dedalus Euro Shorts
General Editor: Mike Mitchell

Dedalus Euro Shorts is a new series. Short European fiction which can be
read from cover to cover on Euro Star or on a short flight.

Sophie Jabès

Alice, the Sausage

Translated by Catherine Petit and
Paul Buck

Dedalus

Dedalus would like to thank The French Ministry of Culture in Paris and Arts Council England East for their assistance in producing this book.

Published in the UK by Dedalus Ltd, Langford Lodge, St Judith's Lane, Sawtry, Cambs, PE28 5XE
email: info@dedalusbooks.com
www.dedalusbooks.com

ISBN 1 903517 51 6
ISBN 9781 903517 51 2

Dedalus is distributed in the United States by SCB Distributors, 15608 South New Century Drive, Gardena, California 90248
email: info@scbdistributors.com   web site: www.scbdistributors.com

Dedalus is distributed in Australia & New Zealand by Peribo Pty Ltd, 58 Beaumont Road, Mount Kuring-gai N.S.W. 2080
email: info@peribo.com.au   www.peribo.com.au

Dedalus is distributed in Canada by Disticor Direct-Book Division, 695 Westney Road South, Suite 14 Ajax, Ontario, LI6 6M9
web site: www.disticordirect.com

Publishing History
First published in France in 2003
First Dedalus edition 2006

Alice la saucisse © copyright Editions Gallimard 2005
Translation copyright © Catherine Petit and Paul Buck 2006

The right of Sophie Jabès to be identified as the author of this book and of Catherine Petit and Paul Buck to be identified as the translators of this work has been asserted by them in accordance with the Copyright, Designs and Patent Acts, 1988.

Printed in Finland by WS Bookwell
Typeset by RefineCatch Limited, Bungay, Suffolk

THE AUTHOR

Born in Milan in 1958, Sophie Jabès's childhood and adolescence was spent in Rome, before travelling the globe. She has worked in television, and currently lives in Paris. Her second novel, *Caroline assasine*, was published in France in 2004 and her third, *Clitomotrice*, in 2005.

THE TRANSLATORS

Catherine Petit is a Belgian born French translator who has translated for Dedalus *Alice, the Sausage* with her husband, the writer and artist, Paul Buck.

They have recently translated *Pierre Klossowski, Catherine Breillat* and an *Anthology of French Erotic Writings* by women.

1

In the beginning were Alice's legs. Slim. Stream-lined. First class. Aristocratic. Without an ounce of fat. Elegant legs, really smooth and soft. Legs that gleamed like satin in the sun. Legs of a gazelle. Delightfully shaped calves and thighs that leapt upwards, uninhibited, without restraint or shame. Legs that streamed towards a flat stomach, firm and hard, a stomach that wasn't one. More of a hollow between the sides and beneath the gener-ous and well-shaped breasts. Slender arms, almost endless, and fragile wrists that one barely dared to touch for fear of breaking them. Alice had a dream of a body which made all the young men hanging around the Termini Station have a hard-on, as well as those sipping a *cappuccino* to distraction in the Piazza Navona.

Alice gave them all a hard-on, the young brown-haired men, the old curly-haired ones, and those stuffed with *pasta alla carbonara* and *penne all'arrabbiata*. The blond men looked at her too, perched on their scooters, eyes riveted on those breasts and thighs that they would have liked to take far away.

Alice didn't allow anyone to touch. Looking was permitted, touching, not. She alone had the right to caress the soft firm skin that she admired for hours in front of her mirror. She scrutinized every nook and cranny and she had to admit she found her body perfect, absolutely perfect. She was especially fond of the gap between her thighs, the curve of her calves and the colour of her nipples, reminiscent of marron glacé. However hard she looked, everything was in the right place, as if blessed by the hand of God.

Alice took care of her body with unadulterated delight. She bought ginger lotions and body butter with orange flower, cinnamon or jasmine. Every morning she spread it on with passion and meticulousness. Sometimes, on summer evenings, she mixed sugar and lemon to make a paste that she used for depilation. With unmatched patience she hunted down every single hair. Everything had to disappear. The paste stuck to her skin and hurt Alice when she had to remove it. The result was sumptuous. Silk and satin. And nobody to benefit. Nobody to caress it. Nobody to come closer. Nobody to breathe her in and be intoxicated.

Alice was not bothered. On the contrary. She had decided a long time ago it would be that way. She was keeping herself for the one and only, the one she would choose to offer her skin to, that skin she cherished every single morning. For him, the man she couldn't imagine. She just knew that one day he would come and she would offer him the splendid body that was hers.

In the meanwhile, she arrogantly ignored the sneering whistles of the young Romans as she passed in her stripy tank tops barely coming down to the golden expanse of her stomach. She went by, haughtily, without a word, without a glance. Only her thighs seemed to smile and whisper tenderly: "catch me if you can."

The Roman boys let her slip by, they didn't

dare to approach her, they preferred to follow the plumper, the less perfect, the more accessible.

Alice liked to walk in the streets of Rome. In fact, the calls of the boys on scooters reassured her. As long as there were men to call after her, she knew she was being looked at and she knew she existed.

2

What Alice liked above all were her feet. She could stare at them all day, admire their arches, their little pointed tips. Alice gave them a languorous massage every evening after having worked at them in a frenzied fervour with a pumice.

It was true, Alice's feet were not lacking in charm. Each was tiny, narrow to perfection, with a cute arch. Fairy feet, she kept telling herself.

For those feet Alice was quite extravagant, with golden court shoes in lizard skin, leather sandals with wedges and laces, open-toed sandals in all colours, two-tone boots in calf. Her shelves were filled with pink, green, purple, mauve, white and blue espadrilles, flip-flops with flowers attached, mules with and without heels.

In the evening she opened all her cupboards

and contemplated her treasures. Nothing was too beautiful for those feet she venerated.

When she went out she took her time before choosing the colour, shape, and height of the shoes for that day. She always preferred high heels, which made her ankles ache. That, thought Alice, gave her some style.

In the streets of Rome she strutted, swinging her hips, and the Roman boys whistled. She was the happiest of women.

In the morning Alice arrived at the library of the Dominican school and waited, her heart beating, for a compliment on her new shoes. When finally it came, she stammered, smiled shyly, almost apologizing, filled with pleasure.

Alice had found that job as a librarian after reading literature at university, studies she had hurried through with little conviction. The place was quiet and restful, sisters in black veils and white dresses slid silently across the shiny marble floor, lowering their eyes and blushing when the priest passed by.

Alice liked to be in that cocoon, for it reminded her of her childhood, her years as a student sheltered in the boarding school on the Via Nomentana.

She felt protected, she felt secure. Once there, she knew she was out of reach of the greedy desires of the Roman boys and the throbbings of their scooters. She enjoyed the absolute silence, the quiet and idle days which left her with enough time and indulgence to check if her skin was still as smooth, her thighs as perfect, her complexion as clear and fresh as ever.

To go to the convent she obviously dispensed with the stripy shorts, opting instead for a long navy blue skirt and a white poplin shirt. She also wore a garnet-coloured headband which made her look like a Madonna. The cook called her Mona Lisa.

Alice lived alone. Her mother, a hair-brained actress who spent her life touring, sometimes phoned her between shows and sent her red roses for her birthday. With each bouquet, Alice wiped away a few tears, full of admiration for her absent and capricious mother who gave her a detailed account of all her amorous adventures through-out the world.

Alice's father was an eccentric with long grey hair who had settled in Athens with a Croatian woman he had met on a Nile cruise. He smoked, he drank, he had seen it all, he had done it all. Alice held her father in veneration, a feeling mixed, though, with a terror whose exact origin she knew nothing about. His loud voice perhaps, his unchallengeable way of imposing home truths, the absolute impossibility of discussing any matter with him.

Alice loved her father but she didn't see much of him. He visited Rome once or twice a year, for Christmas or Easter, breezing through, to buy some *Baci Perugina*, he used to joke.

When he called, Alice prepared as if for an amorous assignation. She donned her most beautiful shoes, her tightest T-shirt, her most low-cut top. She prepared her skin and her hair, her heart was beating so much at the idea of seeing him again . . . Often Alice's father cancelled at the last minute, his pretext a migraine, or an unexpected meeting, or a phone call from Athens compelling him to go back straightaway. Then she had another six months to wait.

Alice had a few friends she saw around four in the afternoon, when she left the library. Arm in arm they went up the Via del Corso, as far as the Piazza del Popolo, licking ice creams from *Giolitti's*, or to the cinema on Piazza Barberini and shared a pizza near the Trevi Fountain.

What delighted Alice, too, was to meet her brother Tonino who sketched the cheerful faces of tourists and passers-by on Piazza Navona. Alice could spend hours sitting there doing nothing, watching him work. She tipped her ankles and her thoughts left to right and right to left, her mind blank and emptied of all worries. She felt good there, still, with the crowd moving around her. Nobody bothered her, not with her brother protecting her. He looked at her and smiled, from time to time presenting her with a portrait of her slender thighs that he painted passionately. Alice's brother was deaf and dumb, and loved his sister dearly. They touched each other with their fingertips to intimate their secrets. The world was theirs.

3

Alice's life slipped by like that, untroubled, between depilations with hot lemon, ice cream cornets with whipped cream, the dark corridors of the Dominican Sisters' convent and the devouring eyes of the Roman boys who hung around. A tranquil and uneventful life. She was waiting for Prince Charming. He was sure to arrive sooner or later.

One day, however, Alice's life was turned upside down.

It happened on the Feast of the Assumption, on a scorching fifteenth of August. There was nobody on the streets of Rome, other than the garnet-red cassocks of a few hurrying arch-bishops, and some red and sweaty tourists. The Romans had left to tan on the beaches at Fregene and Ostia. Some had opted for the cool of the slopes of Frascati and Castelgandolfo. At the last minute, Alice had cancelled a trip to Port'Ercole, she had already taken too much sun. She preferred to stay home listening to *La Traviata* and watching Raffaella Carra on television.

Alice sipped her iced tea in her two-room flat on Piazza della Minerva. She was swinging her tanned thighs in the Roman light, stretching them in turn, when the phone rang.

That phone call changed her life.

Her heart started to beat very fast, an uncontrollable joy took hold of her. It was her father. He had just arrived in Italy. He had had an argument with his Croatian girlfriend and needed a change of air.

Was Alice free for lunch?

Alice dressed with infinite care, hesitated between a pair of bright green shorts fringed with lace and a black pair in stretch material, and finally chose bermudas in multi-coloured check. She also opted for a pretty top in unbleached cotton, slit at the sides. Alice painted her nails a vivid red and slipped on the golden sandals she had just bought in Piazza Frattina. She applied her make-up carefully and smoothed her unruly hair. Alice wanted to look gorgeous.

They were to meet on Piazza del Pantheon. Alice arrived a quarter of an hour early. Her hands were sweating, her eyelids quivering; each encounter with her father was both a joy and a trial. Children played between the tables. Overweight Americans mopped their brows, searched in their guides for the next church to visit.

Alice's father appeared one hour late, as she was about to leave. When she saw him, radiant despite his pale complexion and tousled hair, she smiled. He didn't kiss her. He never did. He didn't ask how she was. He chain-smoked and unloaded an avalanche of details about his row with his lover. Alice didn't really feel like listening but she didn't know how to stop him. He talked without paying attention to her, as if in a trance, oblivious, providing both questions and answers. Suddenly, vaguely remembering that she was there, he looked at her thoughtfully and said:

"You can't understand."

"Of course I can."

"You're young, you have your whole life ahead of you."

He remained silent for a while and then, with a suddenness that Alice took for lucidity, he adopted a solemn air that terrified her. He took hold of her hand and squeezed it very hard.

"Women, women, women . . . My dear, you're not Marilyn Monroe, so remember, you must be nice, very nice to men."

Alice stared at him, horrified, as if an enormous storm had suddenly unleashed itself inside her head.

"I have to be nice to men?"

"Yes, very nice. If you're a woman, either you're beautiful, or you're nice. You don't have a choice, you understand?"

"No," Alice whispered. She was shaking.

"It's very simple." He took her hands in his again. "Are you cold?" He rubbed her fingers absentmindedly. "You are not beautiful, so you must be . . . nice. I can't find any other word. I mean very nice to men."

Alice's father finished his beer silently and, after a last diatribe against the waiter, left.

19

Alice's world had collapsed dramatically.

She who thought she was the prettiest, the most sophisticated girl, who praised her thighs so highly, thought her waist slim, her breasts perfect, she who never tired of smoothing that skin she felt was silky and velvety, had just heard from her own father's lips that, since she was not beautiful, the only way to reach a man's heart was by being nice.

Nice. That word sounded strange. Insipid. Tasteless. Flavourless. Odourless. Alice wondered what it could possibly mean ... to be nice. What did it mean to be nice to men? Have sex without desire? Do the washing up and cooking? Say yes to everything without batting an eyelid? Anticipate someone else's wishes and forget her own? Smile and cry secretly? Put up with everything?

Alice's father had opened up a black hole in his daughter's belly. A yawning chasm that would be hard to fill. A cavern of anxiety, dark, sticky, terrifying. She, who lived in a world of beauty and perfection was left alone with a plethora of questions gnawing at her stomach.

The wound was gaping and it hurt, it really hurt.

How to treat it?

4

The next day, Alice wanted to phone her father. To make him repeat those words which had, or so it seemed, torn her open. To try to understand.

He had already left the hotel where he hadn't spent the night. She called the station, filled with apprehension. She asked to be shown the register of accidents. There was no trace of him.

She ran here, there and everywhere, and then, worn out, she stayed in her bedroom, prostrate, as if drained of her lifeblood, her stomach in knots.

She had to be nice to men . . . Must she be submissive? Affectionate? Passive? Dependent?

Words unravelled, lost all meaning.

Without thinking, Alice took an apricot and she, who usually picked at her food, devoured a whole kilo. She looked at herself in the mirror.

Her features drawn, she saw herself as dull and lack-lustre. Alice, who'd never doubted her ability to seduce, suddenly found her legs shoddy and sad, useless. What good were those thighs if all you needed was to be nice?

Alice had lost her wonderful self-confidence.

When she walked she kept her head down and her shoulders hunched. She, who used to eye the lads up and down and pass by briskly, holding her head high, now glanced at them furtively, trying to catch their eyes. Alice had taken out her flat pumps, she felt shaky on her heels.

An enormous emptiness settled in Alice's stomach, right in the middle, next to her belly button. She needed to fill it.

Alice bought two ice creams, one for the left hand, and one for the right. One vanilla, the other chocolate. Topped with whipped cream. Alice licked them both but didn't feel satisfied. Alice bought two more, one raspberry, the other lemon. As she ate, she forgot her father, her anguish; she concentrated on the acidity of the raspberry and the tartness of the lemon. She closed her eyes, delighting in each mouthful. And for a while, the time it took to lick her ice creams, she thought she was relieved.

The fear returned, quickly, treacherously. The fear of not being attractive, of not knowing what to do, of not being what she had to be.

Alice remained locked in her room for three weeks. Sinking into an anguish of reflection. With tins of tuna and chocolate truffles that she had delivered from the Piazza Navona. Alice didn't see or talk to anybody for several days. Her sole companion was the noise of the Swiss cuckoo clock, a present from her grandmother. Every half-hour it sounded.

Alice ate.

She swelled.

The Dominican nuns asked her back. Mother Superior phoned to see how she was. Alice said she was not well, that she could hardly talk and walk. The sister hung up, quite moved.

Alice reflected, varied her lunches and dinners. She tried the pizza *napoletana* with basil, tomato sauce and olive oil, the pizza *bianca* without sauce and very salty, the *margherita*, covered with *mozzarella*, the pizza with mushrooms, the pizza with potatoes and rosemary, the pizza with olives, the pie with aubergines and courgettes, and the artichoke fritters.

Alice devoured all voraciously, forgetting for a moment the gaping wound she was dressing with *provolone*, parmesan and strained *ricotta*. Nothing satisfied her. Neither the *tramezzini* with ham, nor those with hard-boiled eggs, nor the slices of bread covered in *mascarpone*, or Nutella, nor the *gnocchi* with rosemary, nor those with tomato sauce. Each time she tried a new flavour, she hoped to find an answer to her anguish. Wanting to fill the intense emptiness in her being with *penne* and *pappardelle*.

Sometimes she looked at the men passing under her windows and, leaning dreamily on her elbows, she finished eating her *suppli alla mozza-rella*, thinking about the unbearable futility of things. Indifferent to the racket in the street, she licked her greasy fingers, trying to appease the fear that had bored a hole right through her, there, right in the centre, mid-way between her heart and the top of her thighs.

5

Between two greasy thoughts and three chocolate-coated anxieties, Alice thought it was about time to call her mother, though she was sceptical about the usefulness of such a step. She knew her mother was frivolous, superficial and unfeeling. But Alice had to talk. To pour out her heart. To get rid of doubt and temptation. To find answers to her questions. About her beauty, her body, her soul, the course to follow. Alice felt her life wavering. Her mother, who was on her third face lift and thirtieth lover, could perhaps help.

Alice's mother had been touring Asia for several months. Alice phoned her. She left messages. Her mother did not call back. Alice finally located her in a luxury hotel in Djakarta.

"Darling, what a surprise to hear your voice! Is everything okay?"

Alice remained silent. Her mother's indifference froze her.

"Yes, everything's fine."

Words stuck in her throat. She couldn't speak. The anxiety was there, wedged between her chest and the bottom of her chin. She tried to push it out. To no avail. Nothing came out.

"Is it sunny in Rome? There's been terrible storms here for three days now."

Alice shuddered. Her life was at stake and her mother was going on about the weather.

"I'm afraid at night. All that water panics me. It's like the end of the world." She chortled. "Luckily I've just met a Malayan, rather well turned."

She stopped talking.

"You're not shocked, are you? I know you're broadminded."

Alice was choking. Her mother was about to describe her latest conquest when Alice needed her help, her advice.

"A splendid man, with shoulders to take your

breath away." Alice was holding hers. "He kisses like a god, which is a bonus, of course. Alice, Alice, are you listening to me?"

". . ."

"Alice?"

"Yes."

"I'm not so scared at night. Not with him."

She chortled again. Alice was collapsing. She could barely articulate.

"Mum . . ."

"Don't call me Mum. You know it makes me feel old. It upsets me. You're my little sister. I'm your friend."

"I want to ask you . . ."

"What? You sound terrible. Nothing serious? If it's money, don't ask. I don't have any. Not a penny. Better ask your father."

"I wanted to know . . ."

"Yes?"

Alice remained silent.

"Hurry up. The show starts in an hour and my hair's not even done."

"Mum, tell me the truth. Do you find me ugly?"

Alice had finally decided to say it. She awaited the answer, as vulnerable as a little girl.

"Ugly? But who put those ideas into your head? Are you still depilating?"

"Yes."

"Even your arms?"

Alice sighed.

"Yes."

"And your moustache?"

"Yes."

"You still take care of your feet?"

"Yes."

"You eat enough? You're not too thin?"

"Yes."

"Then everything's okay. Don't worry. Sorry, I have to leave you. My Malayan has just arrived." She whispered: "I'm going to enjoy myself."

Alice hung up. She wiped away a tear or two. Opened three bars of chocolate that she devoured. Peeled four oranges which immediately disappeared into her stomach, which suddenly distended. Took the tops off five cokes that she poured down her parched throat.

Alice regretted having called her mother.

When all was said and done she had bothered her for nothing basically.

All she had to do was to continue eating and everything would be fine . . .

6

Alice was awaiting her turn in the grocery shop near the Via della Rotonda. The *rosette* were cooked to perfection. The *mortadella* was even more pinkish and tempting than usual. The *gorgonzola* looked fresh. The *ricotta* didn't look bad either. A hand on her shoulder made her forget her desire for fine-sliced smoked ham for a minute.

"Pauline!"

"Alice."

A stocky woman almost two metres tall, eighty kilos minimum, whitish skin and platinum blonde hair, with green almond eyes and a bit dumb-looking stood there. Alice hadn't seen Pauline since their last year at senior school.

"I'm just passing through Rome."

"Where do you live?"

"In Corrèze. I keep sheep."

"You've married a shepherd?"

"Yes."

Alice and Pauline burst out laughing. In a flash they both remembered their dreams of Prince Charming, their fairytale hopes. Alice looked at Pauline's calloused hands.

"Are you happy?"

Pauline took her by the arm.

"I'll tell you later."

"*Signorina*, what would you like?"

The grocer's white shirt was looking at them in an inviting manner. Alice leaned towards Pauline.

"Are we eating together?"

"Don't know . . ."

"Come on . . ."

"I could never say no to you."

Alice bought everything she had seen. The *ricotta*, the *mortadella*, the *rosette*, the *gorgonzola*, and also some Parma ham, *grissini*, green olives, anchovies, *mozzarella*, pizza *bianca* and pizza *rossa*.

"I live alone, not far from here."

They walked, carefree, on the paving stones of Rome, bathed in the first rays of spring.

They climbed the dark staircase, laughing. Arm in arm, they opened the heavy door to Alice's two-room flat and, carried away by the warmth and their memories, they gulped down bread, cheese and cold meat as they chatted.

Alice had found a lightness again, she hadn't felt like that for a long time. Pauline spoke non-stop, talking nonsense, being rude, insulting her arse of a husband, swearing that men were all stupid asses whom she was nevertheless fond of, especially when they were good lovers.

Alice was delighted. This woman, she thought, doesn't care about being nice. Life is enough for her.

"Do you remember?"

"What?"

"When the sisters used to say that making love was nothing but skins rubbing together?"

Alice smiled.

"Yes."

"We need . . ." Pauline shrieked with laughter.

"We need to tell those good sisters that skins rubbing together is not that bad. You're still as beautiful, as slender. Haven't you found yourself a fiancé?"

"Not yet."

Alice looked down.

"I've put on weight."

Pauline came closer.

"Not at all. Perhaps your thighs are a bit plumper . . ."

Pauline stroked her legs.

"You look more real. Why so down? With legs so perfect, you could have Rome at your feet."

"You think so?"

"Of course. You want to try? We can go for a walk on the Corso and you'll bring back the man you want."

"Yes, but after I'll have to keep him."

"Who's talking about keeping him? I'm talking about making the most of it, enjoying yourself!"

Pauline was slightly tipsy. Her cheeks were pink.

"And you, out there in the countryside, do you make the most of it?"

"So so." Pauline burst out laughing. "I make up for it here. But, you know, my shepherd, he's not that bad a lover. Not in a sophisticated way, more the powerful type."

Alice looked at Pauline. She was stocky, firm and strong, unattractive, with big hands and a dumb look. Perhaps deep down she was very nice.

"You see, I was wondering, talking about men . . ."

"What?"

"Is it enough to be beautiful?"

"Oh no, sweetie, that's not enough."

"So?"

Pauline stopped, suddenly serious.

"You need to be imaginative."

Alice didn't dare speak.

She didn't know where to start. To reveal her conversation with her father? To share her distress with Pauline? She was afraid she might look ridiculous. How could that two metres tall lump understand her anxiety? Her questions? Life seemed so simple for her. So clear.

"Do you remember my father?"

"Your old man? Of course, he's quite a man."

"What do you mean?"

"He knows a lot about women, if you understand. A funny chap."

Alice looked at her, bewildered.

"Can you repeat that?"

"Don't act the innocent. I repeat what I said: he knows a lot about women, that's all."

Alice couldn't imagine Pauline with her father. That image disgusted her. She would have liked her big enormous mouth to stop uttering so many obscenities.

"You're making that up."

"Not at all. Look at her pretending to be offended. I said nothing. I didn't describe how he fucks, how he caresses, how he makes you come. I just explained that he's a true connoisseur, and you get on your high horse."

Alice started screaming.

"Stop it!"

She seized the pile of plates left on the table and smashed them to pieces.

"You don't understand anything. Anything at all."

She collapsed on the sofa and burst into tears.

"Don't put yourself in such a state, you little shrimp. He's not a saint, that's all. He's a man who eyes anything that moves. As I'm sure you've noticed."

"No. I hardly ever see him. And when I do, it's as if I'm transparent."

Alice was sobbing.

"All fathers are the same. Don't worry, he's just an old bugger. But you, you're a real sweetie."

Pauline stopped for a moment. She had taken Alice in her arms and comforted her as if she was a child.

"Do you remember?"

"What?"

"When you had the prize for being nice, at the convent?"

Alice jumped.

"For being nice?"

"Everybody was gobsmacked. You'd just arrived at the school and they handed you that prize. It was the first time they gave it. And the last."

"Why me? I've forgotten all about it."

"You listened. You never judged anyone.

37

Always obliging. You opened your ears and your heart."

Alice drank in Pauline's words. She held the key. She asked point-blank:

"Is that what it means to be nice to men?"

Pauline answered with a sense of seriousness.

"No. That's not enough. Men want you to open your legs . . . and your mouth too," she added, laughing. "You're going to get cross again."

"No, tell me," Alice just managed to whisper.

"There's nothing to tell. You have to listen to them, make them feel they are important. Give them the *ice cream cornet trick* from time to time."

"Ice cream cornet trick?"

"Come on, enough talk. I'll buy you an ice cream at *Giolitti*'s. That'll change the subject."

7

The air was mild. The Roman girls had taken out their big gypsy earrings in plated silver. They had gone straight from wearing fur coats to wearing low-cut T-shirts and platform shoes. Alice soaked up the ochres and reddish-browns of the Roman façades. On Pauline's arm, she forgot the call of the pizzas and *calamaretti* fritters.

Giolitti's was absolutely crowded. Everybody was in a rush to savour their first ice cream of the summer. Alice recognized the aroma of fresh cream and ground hazelnuts. She thought she could detect raspberry and lemon too. Pauline gave in to a double vanilla-chocolate cornet with cream, Alice to an apricot and orange cornet.

Pauline whispered to her with a laugh:

"I love it. Don't you find it sensual? I mean . . . the ice cream cornet?"

Alice lowered her eyes.

"Do you really only think of that?"

"Eating, fucking, it's much the same, don't you think?"

Alice, who had never seen things from that angle, did not answer. They walked up the Corso in silence. Alice hid behind Pauline, who eyed up the dark-haired men shamelessly. A certain Mauro decided to approach the pair. After exchanging a few words, Pauline followed him, winking at Alice as she left.

"See you soon, darling. Remember, men are like cherries. You take one, the next follows, then a third and a fourth. It just keeps rolling and it's difficult to stop after that."

Alice went back to *Giolitti's*. This time she bought, as usual, two cornets, one for the right hand, the other for the left, licking raspberry then lemon in turn, a to-and-fro that she seemed to enjoy for the first time.

Alice went back home. Without hurrying. She didn't have much to do. She would not go back to the library. She had to discover the meaning of life. She thought about her past alleged niceness, about her father, about all the men to seduce, about all the *gnocchi* to devour, about all the *ice cream cornet tricks* to organize. And in a whirl of tomato sauce with basil, chocolate fondants, vanilla sugar and grilled polenta, she fell asleep, rocked by the breeze, the zooming of the scooters and the shouts of the passers-by.

Nice . . .

8

Alice awoke in the morning with a heavy heart and an empty belly. The almond trees were in full bloom, but she was impervious to the caress of spring. Fear gnawed at her. Fear of failing to understand what men really expected of her.

To be nice, perhaps, but what for?

To be nice . . . meaning to submit, to abandon her own desires? Her aspirations? To renounce living for herself and only respond to the desires of others? To be attentive only to the pleasures of men? To spread her legs, do the dishes and wait . . .

Alice set off for the Corso on her scooter, intent on figuring out men better. Where before she avoided their gaze and sped past with a haughty smile and head held high, now she stared, trying to identify in their often empty eyes, what could justify her niceness. She let them follow her, call after her, hesitating though to go as far as to bring them up to her bedroom.

One day, a blond guy with brown eyes asked if she would give him a lift. Alice was nice, she didn't refuse. She asked him where he wanted to go. He said he didn't know. He'd found her attractive and just wanted to spend some time with her. That was all. Alice thought he was lying. He couldn't possibly find her attractive. That matter was settled. Her father had said so. She was not pretty and could never be.

She decided to take the man to Ostia. The weather was fine. She felt the force of the wind on her face and the tremors of the man behind her. They didn't talk. He was sitting up close, clinging to her without saying a word. In this new warmth, Alice forgot her destiny, her fear, the wound deep down in her belly.

They soon left Casal Palocco behind. She seemed to float among the pines. She sensed him edging closer and slowly realized that by allowing him to do so, she was becoming nicer and nicer.

They never reached the sea. Alice swept into the pine forest just after Fiumicino. They stopped amid the pine needles. Alice removed her shoes, the man too. He sat her down next to him. She could smell garlic and chopped parsley on his breath. Alice didn't remark on it, that wouldn't have been a nice thing to do.

She was wearing a peasant skirt in orange cotton. He began to caress her. His hand crept beneath the folds. Alice said nothing, she wondered how far his hand would go, how far she would let it go. She wanted to see how far she could take her niceness with this man she had picked up on the Corso and who smelt of sautéed mushrooms. The pines looked at her and smiled. Alice thought she could hear them sing. A blackbird was whistling on a broken branch. She felt herself swelling and calming beneath the warmth of his fingers. She decided he was a cook or a pizza seller, for the smell of garlic and parsley was so strong.

She couldn't help thinking that on her return she would buy a pizza *margherita* and a ham *calzone*.

44

Alice was still lost in thought, between fresh tomato and basil, while the man was already penetrating her conscientiously. She could vaguely feel something hard coming and going inside, but she was elsewhere, with the tomato sauce, the green pepper and thyme, the thin slices of marinated mushrooms, the crisp pastry and the oozing sauce.

The man withdrew and lay down beside her. Anxiety returned. She had to eat, and straightaway. They left for Ostia at once. In a restaurant near the sea, she devoured fried scampi and squid with an ecstatic smile. Thinking he was responsible for her blissful state, the man took her hand and asked when they could meet again.

Alice hesitated. He was neither handsome, nor ugly. He didn't look very bright. She even noticed he had a squint in his right eye. She shouldn't push him away. She had to learn.

She thought of her father, his Croatian girlfriend, the sisters and the fine meal she had just finished.

Tomorrow, around ten. Or ten thirty. Alice gave the man her address, dropped him outside the underground and was away on her scooter.

9

Alice awoke at dawn. She wanted to look her best. She removed every unwanted hair. The sweet lemon paste stuck to her legs. It pulled at her skin, which became smooth and soft ... She took a shower. A long shower. Long enough to dream and purify herself. She coated her body with orange blossom lotion and put on her make-up. The cuckoo sounded eight.

She began her wait. The windows were open. She could hear the scooters in the street and the delivery men bumping into passers-by. Two hours left to wait.

She ate.

Croissants filled with cream and some *ciambelle* – sugared fritters with a hole in the middle. Fresh pineapples and chocolate tarts. Rum babas and Neapolitan *stracciatelle*. Petits fours with strawberries and crystallized apricots. She made herself two cups of *cappuccino*. It was nine o'clock. She called the library to inform them she couldn't come to work. Lying made her feel exhausted. She rushed to the bar in the Piazza della Rotonda and devoured two *pizzette* with *prosciutto cotto*. The melting softness of the *mozzarella* reassured her a little.

She was no longer certain she wanted to see that guy again. She could find better. She was bright, her mother, after all, had never told her she was ugly. Pretty neither, mind. Why open her legs and her door to the first comer? Behind the window of the bar, two *rosette* with *mortadella* remained on a plate. She asked for them. She paid and nibbled at them in the street. Alice was very fond of the consistency of the *rosette* bread. No crumbs. A crispy crust, which was easy to tear at bit by bit.

On her way home, Alice realized with relief that it was past ten. Perhaps he was not going to come?

She looked in the fridge. She had to go shopping, it was almost empty. A few olives with chillies and the remains of stuffed courgettes. Someone rang at the door. It was him.

This time Alice found him plain ugly. He had swapped his leather jacket for a three-piece suit.

"Let's get on with it!"

He didn't have much time. He had come to see Alice between two customers. He was a rep for a socks firm and was visiting shops in the area.

He didn't caress her. He penetrated her straightaway and withdrew almost immediately, with bright red cheeks and a shiny glans. It looked like a strawberry and lemon ice cream. He made to get dressed. Alice couldn't resist. That flavour tempted her. She lowered her head and started to lick.

"But . . . but, I've an appoint . . ."

It was slightly bitter, but a new flavour. Alice licked and licked and the man stiffened again, trembling with excitement. He held her head. She took it in her mouth full of sugar, *mortadella*, strawberries and cream. It was a strange ice cream which did not melt. Alice was delighted. She would have liked to stay like that and carry on licking for the rest of her life, without having to lift her head and meet those crooked eyes.

He made her job easier. When he had come he left without a word, slamming the door behind him.

It was only later that Alice discovered he had left fifty thousand lire on the chest of drawers. She went out immediately to buy herself an ice cream cake and two bottles of Chianti.

10

When she returned home, totally excited at the idea of drinking to her new lover's health, Alice finished the two bottles in one go. As for the ice cream cake, it wasn't long before only a few crumbs of iced chocolate were strewn across the plate. Alice smiled. She experienced a feeling of satisfaction, though she didn't know if the contentment was related to the *ice cream cornet* session, the syrupy taste of the nectar, or even the fifty thousand lire which had allowed her to enjoy that impromptu little meal.

That impression of fullness didn't last long. Under the dubious effect of the alcoholic vapours, Alice felt herself staggering. From within. A swirl. A strange oscillating in her belly. Waves in the pit of her stomach. A beast had come to settle there, searching for its place. Winding and unwinding in the empty space. Stretching out fully before nestling above her belly button. Helpless, Alice was a spectator to the twists and turns of the animal. She looked in dread as her belly swelled, but couldn't see anything. The beast was coiling and uncoiling in a kind of quick waltz. It finally decided to resurface, along the oesophagus, undulating more than ever, pushing towards the exit. Alice spewed. The acidity of the stream burnt her throat. Exhausted, she threw herself on the living-room sofa.

Alice had already put on a lot of weight. She had difficulty walking. Going as far as the couch seemed an insurmountable task; at each step she thought she wouldn't manage it.

She only aspired to one thing: sleep. To wrap herself in that soft cotton wool that she wanted to be reassuring. To forget her father, her shoddy lover, her crazy mother. The sisters, the phone-calls to make. To dive into a hole and plunge head first into an endless vertigo. She pulled her legs up as far as her chin. She made herself tiny. The fear had returned and didn't want to let go.

It was a massive fear, an enormous lump in her stomach, something dreadful. Her heart was certainly going to give way. Alice tried to think about precise details, simple facts which could connect her back to reality. The brown of the jacket of the stranger she had picked up on the Corso, the pine needles of the previous day, the caress of the wind in the pine forest, the smell of garlic and chopped parsley, the flannel of the three-piece suit, the acid taste of the *ice cream cornet*, the fifty thousand lire. That money, the symbol of a job well done, a mission accomplished, which had made her feel so fulfilled at first, now tortured her.

Why those fifty thousand lire? She hadn't asked for anything. What was it in her attitude that could have made him think she was expecting payment? That he had to give her some money? Had she hurt him? Had she shown a sign of weariness? Or disgust? How should she interpret that gesture? Was the man satisfied and rewarding her? That's what she had thought until now. She had been so nice that he wanted to offer her something. But if that was the case, why did he go without a word? Why leave money, which is a hurtful act after all? Did he want to make sure he could come back since he had paid?

Or did the money signify, "You're nothing but a whore, you no longer interest me?"

Alice was convinced that she hadn't given enough, that she should have asked if he wanted something more. She should have held him back, talked to him, inquired if he was satisfied. She had been selfish, to lick him like that without looking at him. It was not niceness but off-handedness. He must have thought he was being manipulated, used. With the fifty thousand lire he was re-establishing his superiority. You haven't taken anything. You have given me something. And I pay you for what you gave me.

But then, if she had given something, did that mean she was on the right path, she had started to understand men, to satisfy them?

Questions crowded in Alice's head, crammed in a confusion she couldn't fight. She clutched at one single word: nice. She had to know how to be nice. Her father was staring at her, grinning. She finally fell asleep, having resolved, as soon as she was up, to seek new ways on Piazza Navona to express how irrevocably nice she could be.

The man never came back.

11

Alice left early in the morning. She stopped at the café at the corner of Via della Rotonda. She drank two cups of *cappuccino* and devoured three or four apricot jam *ciambelle*. With her tongue she collected the sugar from the corners of her mouth. She concentrated on that movement, as if her life depended on its success. Men looked at her.

She had put on still more weight. She no longer had a wasp-waist and slender legs. Her calves were curved, her thighs heavy, and her breasts swollen. She had become more accessible. It seemed there was an emptiness to be filled in that flesh which offered itself. Even the most timorous were enticed by that tongue which sought the grain of sugar in the corner. Alice's skin glowed, smoother and more stretched than ever.

Alice could feel the men's gaze on her ankles and her breasts, moulded into T-shirts a bit too tight. She let them approach and smell her. She remained imperturbable, focused on the sugar of the *ciambella* and the froth on the coffee. Some didn't dare talk to her, others sometimes plucked up courage to come close at the bar. Alice could smell their breath, but she didn't lift her head. She didn't want to let herself be influenced; she needed to be nice to all men.

They soon understood her extreme availability, the ease of opportunity. And, without much discourse or much ado, they found themselves in the flat with Alice, who took them there readily.

It was always the same ritual. The quick in-and-out, done more or less well, followed by an *ice cream cornet trick* or two. It all depended on the days and the man's generosity too.

Alice no longer worked at the library, the sisters had finally tired of her. She decided instead to make the men pay fifty thousand lire for every *cornet trick*. The money allowed her to treat herself to every pizza and pasta she dreamt of, the delicacies at *Sabanti's* and visits to *l'Eau Vive* or *la Sacristie*.

The men paid with good grace. Alice had now mastered the art of the *cornet trick*. None regretted it. They went home, some with a taste of whipped cream, others with flavours of honey and orange, essences of mint, rosemary and thyme, the scents of raspberry or lemon with hazelnuts. They all left with a moving recollection of that soft and sweet mixture into which they had plunged with delight.

It was not long before Alice was known throughout the whole neighbourhood. Her reputation swept across the Tiber. They flocked from Trastevere, Nomentana, the rich districts, Parioli, Cassia and the Aventine to savour her favours.

Alice was worn out. After each visit she wolfed down a dozen slices of *mortadella* as well as four or five plates of tomatoes with *mozzarella* and basil she had prepared earlier.

Alice couldn't say no. Some days she didn't have the time to go out. How could she do her shopping? As soon as the man left, the wound in her stomach reopened and needed to be dressed. She had to eat without delay. Alice couldn't wait.

The pain was too strong. At times, she was getting ready to go down to the grocer's when a second male arrived, followed by a third, and a fourth. They all wanted the same thing. Alice gave it willingly.

Her hunger was for ever increasing. The emptiness was enormous, gaping, a big black hole that needed to be filled.

Alice had an idea: on top of the fifty thousand lire, the men would have to bring her sweet things and savoury nibbles. Enough to save time and relieve her pains.

At the beginning the men found the idea delightful. One brought spiced olives, another some *Baci Perugina*, a third *calzone* with ham and cheese. All knew Alice enjoyed good food and performed wonders when she had eaten.

Alice got into the habit of tasting those treats during the *cornet tricks*. One mouthful of *cornet*, one mouthful of pizza, one mouthful of *cornet*, one mouthful of pizza. And so on. The men had never seen anything like it before, a woman sucking them off while stuffing herself. Some found the game funny and exciting. Others took offence.

She didn't take them seriously. She made fun of them. Others questioned their ability to satisfy her. She needed to eat at the same time because she didn't feel anything. "You don't understand," Alice's supporters protested. "She accumulates pleasures. It's by mixing flavours that she reaches ecstasy."

Conversations went on and on at the café. Those who had never tried Alice couldn't wait to claim their turn between her lips in order to give their opinion on the matter.

12

Alice scarcely left her flat now. She sometimes stayed for four or five days at a stretch in her armchair receiving the Roman men. When the dishes they brought were insufficient, she had food delivered. To avoid paying the costs, she came to an arrangement. The delivery men could benefit from her art as long as they forgot about the extras. Alice had always been a very organized young woman. Often, they added a bottle of wine, a pot of honey, some grilled aubergines. They saw Alice's eyes widen, her skin shiver, her mouth gape with pleasure at the sight of the food. They knew they had an agreement.

Alice was getting fatter every day.

She had had to abandon her shorts and her tight-fitting T-shirts. She wore big djellabas in various colours that her mother had brought back from her escapades in Tunisia. The Roman air whistled through. She felt free. Men slipped in under the cotton, occasionally losing themselves among the folds of her abundant flesh.

Alice found it hard to bend down to them. She sat enthroned in her chair and they went down on their knees. She leaned her head over slowly and took them in her mouth, a slice of pizza in one hand, the *cornet* in the other.

Alice hadn't given up her depilation with lemon paste. She was so proud of her skin. She devoted entire nights to it. The surface had increased and bloated. The pretty gap between her thighs had disappeared. Her legs touched now, even overlaid each other. Her bottom had become enormous. Her waist no longer existed. Her body, once so fluid, had been transformed into a big block of fat. A flabby ball from which arms stuck out, which seemed to have shortened through the inflation. And all moved in every direction. A kind of undulating jelly.

Alice didn't really see herself. She, who had worshipped her elfin body, looked at that fat as if it was outside her, as if it belonged to someone else.

Inside, she was beautiful. Her soul had remained pure. Her niceness was becoming more and more evident. Did a few kilos too many matter?

Her eyes screwed up into a rectilineal slit in her round face. Her stomach carried her forward.

She had given up buying herself shoes. She walked barefoot on the tiled floor of her flat.

When she went out, she slipped on flat sandals, it was impossible to endure heels now.

Anyway, Alice preferred to stay home. Climbing the stairs had become a torture. She had to pause to catch her breath at every step. Lifting one thigh, then the other, was akin to a punishment. She couldn't breathe.

Her breasts were painful from swelling.

She no longer left her two-room flat and each day cut herself off a bit more from life, from the light.

Alice took up the habit of receiving in semi-darkness. She drew the curtains and closed the shutters. There was a thin streak of light in the room, that was all. The new clients bumped into the furniture and sometimes cursed. The regulars went straight to the target, arms loaded with fennel, *ricotta* and freshly cut ham.

Some, however, grew tired, finding the game slightly repetitive. Others complained about Alice's fat. It took them too long to find her vulva among the folds, as her vulva was disappearing in the thickening accumulation of flesh. They lost patience seeing her stuffing herself instead of concentrating on their member. Alice jeopardized their virility. The darkness . . . the stairs to climb . . . the men became fewer and more cautious. The women had also started to smell those funny odours on their husbands' organs and began to ask too many questions.

Alice's clients were less numerous. Their visits less frequent.

Alice had more time to eat.

She had moved her bed into the kitchen, with the fridge at hand. The days without visitors she stayed in bed, opened the fridge door and helped herself. Alice enjoyed those days. She ate without a fork, without a knife. With her podgy fingers.

The more she ate, the more she felt like eating. She had opened a breach in her stomach. And as she tried to fill it, the opening intensified.

The delivery men found her sprawled in the kitchen and laughed as they took her. It was really easy to fuck in such conditions. No foreplay, no endless conversations. If they were so inclined, there was always the possibility of a *cornet trick*. Alice proposed the 'lying down' approach, and sometimes, without even taking off their helmets, they would place their cornet between Alice's lips without her having to get up. She often had her mouth still full of pasta or *suppli*. The delivery men were delighted. It was a bit of fantasy in their dull lives.

13

It wasn't long before Alice only ever saw the men delivering pizzas. She had less and less money to treat herself to anything else.

She still had three regulars.

Those three came whatever happened, wind or rain. Even if the pope was delivering a sermon in Piazza Santo Pietro, they never missed a session. Those three were unwavering supporters of Alice's *cornet tricks*. None was married, thus they could enjoy the bouquet of flavours offered by Alice without concern.

The first man was called Fabio, the other two, Fulvio and Flavio, were twins.

Fabio was a very refined gentleman in his sixties, always dapper with a top hat that he raised in greeting.

He used to arrive every Wednesday at four thirty. The cuckoo sounded, he entered.

His skin was shrivelled. He had explained to Alice that he had just retired. He was a lawyer from Naples who had never married. Fabio spoke very politely in a measured tone. He didn't have one hair left on the top of his head. When he took his clothes off, he folded each garment carefully on the chair so as not to crease them. He wore long white underpants and shirts in cotton poplin with different cuff-links for each visit.

Alice never received Fabio in the kitchen. That would not have been appropriate. On Wednesday morning she dragged her bed back to her bedroom. That was becoming harder and harder. Sometimes she closed the kitchen door and asked him to make himself at home in the living-room. In the dark she couldn't see his wrinkles and white hair. She could feel his delicate, diaphanous hands, which had never touched the earth, hands which had shrivelled only from contact with paper and books. Alice was in heaven: she was sleeping with an intellectual.

Above all, Fabio was a very generous man. He

gave her a hundred, sometimes two hundred thousand lire, and wasn't slow to understand what made the young woman happy. Thus he arrived loaded with marrons glacés, chocolates, rum babas, walnut bread. He chose the very best cheeses for Alice and refused to even taste them. Trembling, Alice offered him some. Fabio was shrewd, he told her to keep it all, she deserved it.

Those words did Alice's heart good. She did everything he wanted.

Fabio liked to caress her. He took his time. Searched through her folds. Marvelled at her rolls of fat. He talked about the outside world, informed her about politics, inflation and terrorism. Explained to her about the Red Brigade while conducting the usual ceremony to find his way in.

Alice allowed him to proceed. She didn't care how long the session lasted. She knew that Fabio always bought the best marrons glacés and that his ham had been selected in the finest delicatessen.

Fabio was obviously very fond of the *cornet trick*. The first time he had asked, he had stammered shyly, almost whispered. Alice had encouraged him, assuring him that it was her speciality.

Fabio had already been coming for a few months and Alice longed to ask him for permission to savour the marrons glacés during the *cornet trick*. But Fabio was so refined, so polite, she didn't dare.

One day, Fabio read the longing in her eyes and brought her the marrons glacés. For a while Alice forgot to be nice and gave herself up to the marrons and the lawyer's penis, her mouth full of sugar. She even thought she had come once. She was annoyed with herself. She could not let herself go.

She had to concentrate on his pleasure. Perhaps he would stop visiting if she neglected him, if she didn't ask him enough questions . . . The lawyer often repeated that she was a nice girl and proposed that she come and settle in his home in the South.

Alice always refused. She couldn't really understand why, but she couldn't say yes. She didn't want to give up her habits, her cosy bed, her days spent eating and sleeping.

He told her to join him in Naples, where they could see each other every day. He would buy her everything she wanted.

Sometimes Alice was tempted. No longer living alone, no more counting the money and the packets of pasta at the end of the month to be sure to have enough to eat. The offer was tempting. Perhaps Fabio was her Prince Charming after all. Such a distinguished man, one who knew how to choose fresh *lasange* and marzipan.

But she had her doubts when she looked at his wrinkled penis, his shrivelled head, his clothes carefully folded on the chair.

How to introduce him to her father? What would he say? He would make fun. Fabio was so refined, so learned, her father swore every other word. He would probably insult him if he had had too much to drink.

Instinctively, Alice knew it would not be a good idea to introduce him to her mother.

There were also the twins, but Alice had never said a word about them to Fabio. How could she leave them behind?

14

The twins had been a present to Alice.

They had arrived one summer morning, unexpectedly. Alice had just got up and was lazing about on the sofa. The shutters were barely opened. Rays of light streaked the room. It seemed as if there were haloes of dust in the air. Alice was dreaming.

They had stayed in the doorway, shy, their heads bobbing. Alice didn't notice them straightaway. They were hidden in the semi-darkness. They were standing up very straight, hands in their pockets, not daring to come forward. Shy. Awkward. Embarrassed. Alice invited them in. They didn't speak. They looked at her without saying a word. How gorgeous they were! Alice had never seen anything so wonderful! Both had black curly hair and water-green eyes. They were handsome, with strong muscular thighs, square shoulders and narrow waists. Two statues by Michelangelo that had escaped from Florence.

There was, though, something rigid about them. Something indescribable which made them strange. A steadiness in their gaze. An absence. An air of 'we are here', while drifting away.

They didn't say a word. Alice even wondered if they were mute. She slipped between them. They smelt of sea and salt air. Seventeen, eighteen years old, no more. Closely shaven, with patched blue jeans. Alice hesitated. She felt burnt by their beauty. She was suddenly scared. Scared to get attached. Scared of the violence of that attraction for those two divine bodies. It was as if she were discovering a man's body for the very first time. And there were two of them.

She came closer. They didn't move, they seemed terrified. Their rigidity intrigued Alice.

Where did they come from? Who had sent them? Why so early in the morning? Why didn't they speak? Did they know who she was? Had they come for the *cornet tricks* too? Why didn't they demand anything? What exactly did they want?

Absentmindedly, Alice caressed the cheek of one; the other, encouraged by the intimacy of the gesture, decided to speak.

"I am Flavio."

The other followed.

"I am Fulvio."

"I am Alice. Don't be scared. Where do you come from?"

"Manicomio."

"Manicomio?"

They explained that they had just escaped from a mental hospital in Ostia. That they had been wandering in Rome for two days. That they had seen the front door open and come up. And there, at her door, which was not closed, they had known it was fate. They had entered.

Alice didn't believe a word. How could they explain that they were so close-shaven, or that they seemed so neat and clean?

They didn't answer her questions. They just said in unison:

"We are very hungry."

Alice then did something she had never proposed to any of her visitors. She was brimming over with kindness for those two crackpots with the bodies of athletes, who kept smiling at her. She invited them to her table and started to cook.

They sat down. She took out the *ricotta*, the *mortadella*, put water on to boil for the pasta, prepared some *suppli* and creamy scrambled eggs. She re-heated a leftover pizza and the three of them started to eat.

It was the first time Alice had offered to share her culinary appetites. Eating had become a solitary pleasure, almost a shameful one. Fulvio and Flavio attacked the food, vigorously wolfing down everything. Alice was delighted.

"Do you want some more?"

"Yes."

She emptied the fridge. She roasted slices of liver bought the day before, prepared tomatoes with *mozzarella*, offered them the profiteroles that the lawyer had brought her on Wednesday afternoon.

They wolfed it all down. They looked like two children who had come back to their mother after having done something extremely stupid. They had come to seek her forgiveness by honouring her cooking.

It was almost two by the time they finished their meal under Alice's stupefied gaze.

"Was it good?"

"Very."

They added in their mechanical voice:

"Now we are tired."

Alice made them lie down, Flavio on her bed, Fulvio on her sofa. She covered them with blankets, like two big babies.

She let them sleep and took shelter in the bathroom. Alice looked at herself in the mirror. She saw for the first time her bloated cheeks, her double-chin as a bird's ruff, her podgy arms, the folds of her stomach, her flabby bottom. She thought about those two divine men and started crying.

15

The twins came back every morning and, every day, Alice cooked for them. They spoke little. She had finally realized that their story was true. They had really escaped from the psychiatric ward and were living with an old auntie who had taken them in when they were young. The auntie only spoke Sicilian and communicated very little with the outside world. They felt safe at her place. They had lost their parents when very young, mown down in a car accident. They were adamant nobody was ever going to find them. They didn't want to go back there, "to the hostel," as they called it.

Alice was fascinated by the colour of their eyes. She could spend hours contemplating them. As long as they were there, she forgot to eat. Her wound was still raw but merely seeing them fulfilled her. She felt very grateful for those two men who came to see her every day and had never asked for anything yet. They didn't seem to know anything about life, failure, fear or renunciation.

She gave them all the treats the old man brought her, only keeping the marzipan for herself, which she ate greedily once they were gone.

One day, they came earlier than usual. The cuckoo hadn't sounded yet.

They didn't dare enter. Each had a chocolate ice cream cornet in his hand. Alice understood. They must have heard the men in the bar talking about her talents and, mentally defective as they were, they still wanted to take advantage of them.

Alice was nice. Very nice. She was not offended. She made them sit on the sofa and took off their clothes. They sat upright, petrified. She sucked them for a long time, passionately, as she had never sucked before. From time to time she lapped at the chocolate ice creams which had started to melt.

Their eyes rolled, their bodies stiffened.

They came together in her mouth. Alice

thought it was lucky she had put on weight. Perhaps she wouldn't have been able to contain them both in her throat. They thanked her movingly and asked if the meal was ready.

Alice was very fond of them. She liked their simplicity, the straightforward way they said things, their dreamy air, even their tantrums, real children's tantrums. One evening, she had forgotten the smoked ham that Fulvio was particularly partial to. Furious, he had smashed the kitchen windows before curling up on Alice's knees to beg forgiveness.

Alice had found a new purpose in life: to feed the twins and make them discover the pleasures of the flesh.

Soon, they were no longer satisfied with the *cornet tricks*. They wanted to take her in every manner and from every angle.

Alice let them do it joyfully. She ate at the same time. They were all laughing. Flavio penetrated her in front and Fluvio took her from behind, while Alice gorged on minced-meat pies. They licked her, losing and finding themselves in her folds. She spread her legs for those two curlytops who drank her with delight, whispering: "O God, O God."

The twins had never had a woman before. They went crazy with the abundance of flesh Alice offered them generously. They went round and round it, each with his long penis, taking their time, asking for food too. Sometimes the three of them wallowed on the floor, rolling in the crumbs of *bruschetta* and pizza they had just swallowed.

Alice had never had so much fun.

They often ran around on all fours in the flat and, breathless, took her, laughing. Alice had invented a game. She lured them into the kitchen, near the fridge that she opened. They toppled her over and, while one climbed astride her and the other licked her, she stretched her hand out and savoured, one by one, the lawyer's marrons glacés.

That is why, when the old man asked her to join him in Naples, she was reluctant. The financial security tempted her, but she was afraid of becoming bored.

16

It was three o'clock. The cuckoo had just sounded. Alice had spent her day getting ready for the lawyer. Fabio liked Alice's generous flesh but he prefered it groomed.

Alice had depilated her thighs, arms, calves and pubis. The whole operation took her longer and longer. She had varnished her toenails and rinsed her hair carefully. She had sprinkled talc over her body and perfumed it with orange flower water. Rolls of flesh had invaded her body from all sides, her thighs overflowed with fat and her breasts had quadrupled in volume. She knew the old man appreciated the folds and the excess, the swelling of her breasts and the ballooning of her belly, as if it meant he had his money's worth. But *it* had to be clean and smell nice.

Alice slipped on her djellaba with some difficulty. It was becoming too tight. She settled on her sofa with a chocolate and banana sandwich.

The cuckoo sounded four. He would soon be there.

At that precise moment – Alice often thought about that moment which would suddenly accelerate the rhythm of her life – at that precise moment, someone rang the bell. The old man was early, that was not like him. Alice brushed her hair.

A voice was heard shouting triumphantly:

"It's me!"

Alice's bejewelled mother was pirouetting in the doorway.

Alice couldn't believe her eyes. Her mother hadn't phoned her in at least six months. She was popping by, looking extremely well, perched on stilettoes and wearing a Chanel suit, cut perfectly.

"Darling, my darling, how are you? It's dark in here, come closer. Let me look at you."

She spoke loudly, opened the windows, unfolded the shutters. The light of Rome flooded the room.

"Doesn't smell very nice here. Don't you ever clean? Where are you?"

Alice was hiding. She wanted that woman to disappear as quickly as possible. The old man was about to arrive. She had to go. Alice had taken refuge in her bedroom.

"Here, here. I'm not feeling too good."

"You're in bed? In the middle of the afternoon?"

She wouldn't stop her prattling.

"But you've put on weight. How ugly you are!!! You should be more careful. Get up so I can see you."

Alice was paralysed. She wanted to stop that stream of words.

"I have a virus. It's very contagious."

"A virus? That's horrible! I won't come any closer, I'm so weak."

"What do you want?"

"Nothing, nothing. I just came to see how you were. I finished my contract in Korea. I'm spending a few days in Rome. I'm broke. Can I stay with you?"

She frowned and, with a sigh, murmured:

"Though it's a bit cramped in here!"

"No!" Alice had shouted that "no" with all her might.

"Why? Is there someone?"

"Mum, go now, I'm very tired. We'll talk about it tomorrow."

"As you wish. What is that djellaba? It's absolutely dreadful. You look deformed."

"You gave it to me."

"Really?" she exclaimed and, clicking her heels, "I must have made a mistake. It's the one I wanted to give the maid."

"See you."

Alice was worn-out.

"See you tomorrow."

She was finally about to leave when the cuckoo sounded half past four. Alice shivered in horror. She heard the doorbell. Fabio had just arrived.

"Don't get up. I'll open it for you."

Her mother invited the man in. Alice could only hear snatches of their conversation.

"She is very ill, you know. I've been looking after her for a week. Do you know her well?"

Bursts of laughter ... Alice imagined her

mother mincing and twirling around the lawyer.
She sprang out of bed and joined them.

"Here she comes. My God, you are obese! You
were so slender. A woman can't let herself go like
that. What do you think?"

She turned to the lawyer and took his hand.

"We, who understand what life is about," she
lifted the lawyer's hand to her face, "we know how
precious life is. How soft your hand is! It's like a
feather."

Alice saw with horror that he had blushed. Her
mother was flirting with the old man in front of
her. Her most generous lover. The one who could
talk art and politics. The one who was feeding the
twins and brought her the very best marrons
glacés in town. She was trying to seduce him. He
was looking desirously at her and Alice didn't say
a word. She felt she was choking.

Her mother carried on.

"Do you want some tea? Oh, you've brought
some marrons glacés. How refined! How
delightful!"

This time she came closer to the man and
stroked his cheek. Her waist was narrow and her

hips generous. She clung to him. The lawyer turned purple.

"You must be a marvellous man, a man . . ." she stressed the word *man*, as she clung further to him, ". . . a man of taste."

She stepped back straightaway. The lawyer was confused.

"You are?"

"An actress."

Alice opened her mouth for the first time.

"Fabio, this is my mother."

"Your mother!" The lawyer was speechless with admiration. "Madam, you are extraordinary. What a zest for life, what spirits!"

He took her hand and kissed it respectfully.

Then, something incredible happened. Something monstrous, inconceivable. Alice's mother drew in her waist, took a deep breath and, as if it was the most natural thing in the world, grabbed hold of the lawyer's arm.

"Let's go out, shall we? The child . . ." she chuckled, "the child is ill. It's too hot here. You must have so many things to tell me." She whispered in his ear: "I heard it's contagious."

The lawyer didn't resist. He raised his hat to say goodbye to Alice.

"Do have a rest, my dear."

Without another word, they were gone.

In a fraction of a second, Alice's mother had destroyed half of her daughter's world.

Devastated, the young woman collapsed on the sofa. How could he be manipulated like that? Such a fine man. A man who had been promising Naples to her for such a long time. How could he have given up his *cornet trick?* How could her mother have jumped at the opportunity so easily? She had made fun of her, called her plain ugly, treated her like a child!

Alice had not been able to respond. She was petrified. Her mother had stolen her lover from right under her nose and she hadn't said anything, hadn't done anything.

He would be back soon. For sure. Alice tried to convince herself of the man's fondness for her. She was thinking about her mother's hypocrisy, her infinite perversion. He would realize that finally. He would miss Alice's rolls of fat and her hot lips. He would be back.

Alice finished the box of treats brought by the lawyer in a few seconds. That didn't comfort her. She gulped down bread and *mozzarella*, tomatoes and basil, ham and *mortadella*. The pain was still there.

"Why? Why me?"

Three weeks later, Alice's mother phoned. They were living in a flat with a terrace in Pausilipe. They had tied the knot in Capri. They would keep in touch.

Who was going to bring her marrons glacés now?

17

Alice had remained prostrate for hours. Not doing anything. Not moving. Why had he married her, Alice's own mother? Why had he gone off with her?

Why had he left her, Alice? Hadn't she given everything? Hadn't she spread her legs? Hadn't she sucked him as he wanted to be sucked? Hadn't she been nice enough?

How had her mother realized so quickly what he wanted? Why did she know better than Alice? Why hadn't she taught her anything about life?

Alice pictured the lawyer. His clothes carefully folded on the chair. The hours spent listening to him when he caressed her. The *cornet tricks*.

What more could she do?

She had heard her mother, her simperings, the

way she said, "You are a marvellous man," while clinging to him.

It was too late to learn. Her body no longer belonged to her. That shapeless mass she had become couldn't hope for anything.

Alice thought about talking to her father. So that he could free her. So that he could finally explain the essence of life. Men's desire and what he meant by being nice. So she would know the answer, and could share with him her anxieties, her fears, her failure.

She didn't dare. He would laugh. Make fun. He wouldn't understand. She decided to keep quiet. At least for the moment.

She would try again. With the twins. Perhaps she would succeed with them. She would do everything, absolutely everything they asked. She would fulfill their every desire. She would have no other lover. She would devote herself to their pleasure alone. She would have to learn how to satisfy them. Totally.

The wound in her stomach was bleeding. The anxiety was terrible. Like a flood of waves about to submerge her. She would never know. She would never succeed. Powerless, she had witnessed her own mother's little game. The twins would leave too and she would be alone, desperately alone.

Alice dragged herself to the Piazza Navona to find her brother. Her fear was too strong, too overwhelming. She had to share it. She could barely walk. She walked with such tiny steps. Her thighs weighed a ton. She was breathless. The summer heat suffocated her. She paid a boy to support and accompany her to Tonino's easel.

He was painting. When he saw her coming, his face lit up. In the blank look of the deaf mute, Alice forgot her fat, her elephant buttocks, her enormous breasts. She felt light and gorgeous.

He made her sit next to him. He caressed her face, kissed her hands. They cried. He, because he was reunited with her, she, because she could feel somebody's love for her.

He signalled her not to move and started her portrait.

Alice protested, then gave up. She remained motionless, her thoughts fixed, her eyes wet. Nobody looked at her. Men were passing by without even seeing that mass of deformed and weeping flesh. She half opened her slit eyes, buried in the fat, and tried to meet their eyes. It was pointless. She had become invisible. They didn't even suspect there was a soul in that woman's gaze.

Night fell very late. It was ten o'clock. Tonino had finished. He rolled up the canvas and gave it to his sister. He wanted to take her back home.

They struggled along the paved streets of Rome, avoiding the scooters and honking cars with difficulty. The heat had diminished slightly. Alice felt less heavy, and yet very tired.

Her brother kissed her goodbye at her front door. He didn't want to come up. Alice found herself alone in her flat. Worn-out.

She ate. All that was left. Pizza. Pasta with parmesan. A leg of lamb. Some *suppli.*

She drank. Chianti. Coke. Orangina. San Pellegrino.

She threw herself on the sofa. She caught sight of the rolled portrait her brother had presented her with, unfolded it carefully and uttered an astonished, "Oh!"

Her brother had drawn a sausage. An enormous sausage. Round. Appetizing. Perfect. A gigantic chipolata.

So that was what he saw as he was drawing her?

Sausage meat.

He had contemplated her with all the love in the world, but his hand was telling the truth.

Alice looked at herself in the mirror and burst out laughing.

A sausage . . .

18

Alice tidied the portrait away. The twins were coming the next day. There was nothing left in the fridge. And nothing in her purse. She decided to sell her odds and ends: ashtrays bought in Tarquinia, vases from Herculanum and Paestum, ribbons from Sorrento and mats from Amalfi.

Alice sold off everything that could interest the dealers from Porta Portese: the Venetian chandelier she had inherited from her grandmother, the chest of drawers inlaid with bronze an old aunt had given her for safe-keeping, white wicker chairs and a table in wrought iron. She accumulated three hundred thousand lire. Enough to keep her afloat for a few weeks.

She prepared the most extravagant dishes for Fulvio and Flavio: pasta with anchovies, chocolate pizzas, apricot soufflés, frogs in batter. They devoured everything in silence and moved to the bed.

Alice was more and more exhausted. She mostly ate pasta and excessive amounts of sweet pastries, which she couldn't give up. The twins took her in turn, half laughing, half belching. They insisted on the *cornet trick*. Alice hardly had the strength to lift her head to either erect penis, but she never refused. She wanted to go the whole way.

She let them caress her. They licked her fervently, sometimes when they were still eating, in a mix of flavours which delighted them. They would lie down on the table and mix pasta, parmesan, clitoris, tongues and penis in an amazing and jubilant ballet.

Alice looked at them and smiled. She would have liked to make the most of it, but she was elsewhere. Her body no longer belonged to her.

"Did you have a good time?"

They nodded, got dressed, gave her a hug and told her they loved her.

For those words, Alice would have accepted

damnation. Each time she invented new dishes and new games, offering her fat to be shared in a banquet she would have liked to be endless.

One evening, the twins, having just finished a nice meal – aubergines *au gratin* and *porchetta* – asked her point blank:

"Alice, why don't you prepare us sausages? Sausages are nice. We adore them."

"Don't you like my cooking?"

"Yes, we do, but we want sausages, sausages . . ."

The twins repeated, "sausage, sausage" non-stop, like an endless refrain.

Alice thought she was going mad. They didn't stop.

"Sausage, sausage." The words fizzed in all directions. Alice couldn't catch them.

"Why don't you cook us sausages?

Their voices were hissing. They wagged their heads and shouted, "sausage, sausage".

Still screaming, they penetrated her.

"Sausage! Alice is nasty. She doesn't want to make us sausages. Nasty Alice."

Alice's head was about to explode. She had

promised herself she would endure everything, but the twins, flush-faced, were running around the flat stark naked and bawling, "sausage, sausage".

"Stop it!" she was screaming. "You loonies. Get the fuck out of here. Haul your dicks elsewhere. I've had enough."

Alice took hold of a pile of plates and, with what little strength she had left, threw it at the two men. They fled, terrified, clutching their clothes tight.

The door slammed.

What had she done?

19

The twins did not return. Neither Monday. Nor Tuesday. Nor Wednesday. Nor Thursday. Nor Friday. All went by. Saturday too. And even Sunday.

Days and weeks followed each other. They showed no sign of life.

Alice was in despair. She didn't know how to contact them. She wanted to apologize, make them come back, whisper loving words to them. Cook all the sausages in the world for them if need be.

Alice had deliveries of merguez, chipolatas, streaky bacon, dried sausage, *mortadella*, black pudding, white pudding, garlic sausages, spicy sausages and sausages with herbs. Perhaps the smell of sausages would make them come back, she hoped. But they did not reappear.

Alice prayed. Alice cried. She called the local mental hospitals. None had heard of the twins.

She ate the sausages. And swelled wonderfully. She felt lost. There was no man left to desire her. Not even the delivery men who set down their orders quickly, without even a smile.

The room stank. Alice kept the shutters closed. She rarely had a wash, her hair was stuck to her head. Alice lived in the dark. A sluggish darkness. Without hope. Anxiety had taken over the whole room. Despair was turning to fat. Some evenings she was afraid she might burst.

She contemplated her metamorphosis with horror, not knowing how to escape from it.

And then one day the light dawned. Alice, who slept practically the whole day, understood miraculously, between two plates of pasta and a few strings of sausages, what remained to be done.

She should have thought about it earlier. Everything suddenly seemed clear. Her father. Her lovers. The fat. The flesh. Her brother's portrait. The twins.

A sausage, she had to become a sausage. And be ready for the twins' return. They wanted a sausage. She was going to prepare them the most tasty, the most delectable, the most bountiful, the most exquisite of sausages.

She mustn't waste a minute. It was no mean thing to become a sausage.

20

Alice had seen the light: that was it, that was exactly what she wanted to be, a *salsiccia*, a beautiful and big *salsiccia*, extremely fragrant, smooth and fat. A sausage. Alice couldn't take her eyes off the streaky bacon she had just prepared for herself. Alice the sausage. Alice had finally found her way. She was lying there, in the sauce, in the middle of the lentils, smiling, pleasing and appetizing.

Alice went to stretch out on the sofa. The revelation was decisive, she had to meditate, weigh up the consequences of her discovery, establish a plan of action, concoct a strategy. The task was not going to be easy.

Alice dragged herself in front of the mirror. She smiled with childish, amazed delight. Her arms bloated, her stomach, swollen like a wine skin, her eyes drowned in the fat of her cheeks constituted so many pleasant surprises for her to evaluate with thorough precision. Those arms had to swell even more, puff up, stretch and become even podgier. There had to be no more difference between arms and fingers, or between thighs, calves, ankles and feet. All had to come together in one round form towards which all Alice's desire strained.

Alice's skin was soft. She worked at making it even smoother. Three times a day she slid across the floor, on the tiles from Ferrara. She rolled from left to right, right to left, roaring with laughter. It was a long time since she had laughed so much. She liked the contact of the cold floor beneath her thighs and forearms. She kneaded her body in that manner for hours on end. Her skin was turning blue, with red marks, resembling the marbling of the chipolatas bought in the market. Alice was delighted.

Alice was still hoping the telephone would ring. But it didn't. In fact, she was no longer in such a hurry to see the twins again. Deep down, she knew that they would reappear one day, enticed by the fat. She wanted to be ready, surprise them, amaze them, leave them breathless.

Alice had bought a parrot. It was a male macaw which murmured words of love and encouragement all day long. "Go go tootsie wootsie," it hurled when it saw Alice rolling on the floor. "I love you, yeah yeah yeah," it sing-songed with little clucks of satisfaction, delighting the young woman each time she was depilating. The parrot could also sing some tunes from *La Traviata* that he interlaced with obscenities, thus rendering something like, "*E troppo tardi . . .* show us your arse, sweetie." Alice listened to it while eating pizzas, her mouth full and her hands greasy. She spent hours making him repeat, "Alice the sausage, Alice the sausage." The parrot looked at her with empty round eyes and intoned, "Alice the sausage, the girl who fucks nice, Alice the sausage, the girl who sucks spice, Alice the sausage, are you getting the message?"

Alice often fell asleep on the sofa. The parrot carried on muttering "heave-ho!", the cuckoo sounding the hours and half hours, amid the greasy wrappers, the bottles of Chianti and Coke, the piles of plates she refused to wash.

Alice left boxes of pizza, plates with sauce, leftovers of ice cream and squid fritters littered everywhere. It all blended cheerfully, and it stank like a pigsty. Alice delighted in that putrid smell. "A sausage cannot be made with Hermès scarves," she loved to repeat.

Alice slept more and more. She was awake for three hours a day at the very most. She rose, or rather, slid to the floor, crawled as far as the kitchen, devoured everything there was to devour, gave some seed to the macaw, which thanked her with moist eyes: "Thank you, sausage," looked with satisfaction at the progress of her swelling in the mirror and rolled back to bed.

21

Alice's skin became extremely smooth. Flavoured too. With basil. Parsley. Green peppercorns. She smelt of the herbs and spices she sprinkled passionately on her food. It was marvellous to behold. Her flesh was swelling, abundant, springy, or almost.

Alice went to so much trouble caressing herself with creams and potions patiently prepared, kneading herself, that it was as if her skin became lined with felt. Alice had started her depilations again. The sessions lasted longer, that was all. She now needed between ten and twenty kilos of lemons and as much sugar, very little water and lots of patience. Alice had plenty of that.

Every evening Alice inspected the results. Sometimes she lost heart. She collapsed on the sofa and contemplated her bruised legs with sadness. The task seemed impossible, the goal too far away. She cried, leaning on her Regency chest of drawers, ruminating with dread over the idea that she would probably never be a sausage. She looked at her life again. Those men to whom she had been as nice as possible, her father who used to sing in a raucous, albeit melancholic voice, her mother gone with her most generous lover. It all seemed so vain and useless. Her efforts, her sufferings, for nothing. For a few bruises and a few kilos too many.

Her anxiety overwhelmed her all the more. The pit deep in her stomach became more hollow and deeper still. More threatening. She swallowed big plates of *cannelloni*, heaped spoonfuls of chestnut cream and fell asleep like an angel.

Alice always had the same dream. She was on a beach, on the edge of a jetty, and there was an enormous chocolate cake topped with a pretty red cherry on the water. She wanted to get to the cake. A parrot came and landed next to her, cackling in her ear, "Alice the sausage, Alice the sausage." She could see her limbs change form, her legs and arms swell, her body become a big, chubby, white pudding with wings. She could then follow the parrot which took her near the much coveted dessert. As soon as she approached, the dessert sank in the water. As she left, it came back to the surface. The more she desired it, the more it seemed to defy her. She finally made up her mind and shot forward, trying to catch it. She landed a few centimetres from the cake. Only the cherry was left and from up close it looked all wrinkled.

Alice always woke up in a sweat, screaming. She had missed the cake, she had missed her life.

In order to soothe the wound which reopened, she dragged herself towards the fridge, finished off two plates of *lasagne* and a few slabs of milk chocolate. She found some *bocconcini, mozzarella, rosette* with *mortadella* and lentils with bacon.

Slightly calmer now, she went back to bed holding her bulging stomach.

She couldn't fall asleep. The cuckoo sneered. The parrot snored on its perch. Alice felt lonely and empty. With that strange feeling that she was going to take off if she didn't stuff herself. She had to eat.

There was not much left. Alice was acting crazy. Stale farmhouse loaves, old apples that had been left about, roasted chicken legs, slightly rancid. Alice found a tin of flageolet beans at the bottom of the cupboard. Alice hated those beans. She devoured them avidly. It was as if she had a vacuum cleaner in her stomach. She sucked in everything she could find: unsalted rusks, stuffed cabbage, olives, a jar of mustard, some fresh cream, gherkins, slabs of cooking chocolate. Nothing could fill the emptiness.

Alice went back to bed. She dreamt of *porchetta* and grilled lamb chops.

Days went by, nights too.

Alice hardly moved now. She ate straight from the bags the delivery men left at her door. She no longer had the strength to lift them.

She caressed her shapeless body. Weighed its roundness in her hands. Spent hours staring at the portrait her brother had drawn of her. To become imbued with it. Convinced that her wish was soon to be granted.

Alice, the sausage . . .

22

One horrible January morning, a cold, rainy and soulless day, Alice didn't wake up. Perhaps she felt like making the most of her reserves, like hibernating, we will never know, but the fact was that Alice didn't deign to open her eyes. The macaw called in vain, "Sweetie, tootsie wootsie, sausage," but she kept her eyes closed.

It was on that same morning that, with a severe storm breaking outside, the twins chose to push the door open and pay their friend a visit.

At first they were taken aback by the smell. They almost left, but they had brought three kilos of lentils with them, it would have been a shame to leave before showing them to Alice.

So they came in, groping their way in a room plunged into total darkness, whispering:

"Alice, Alice, are you there?"

They couldn't see a thing, the parrot kept quiet. They thought Alice must be out and they would have to wait patiently on the sofa.

When they sat down they felt a kind of viscous but, at the same time, firm mass beneath them. They leapt to their feet.

"What's that?" they shouted, their heads bobbing.

Before their eyes was an enormous sausage, a kind they had never seen. A pink sausage marbled to perfection, a magnificent sausage.

"What a beauty!"

The twins had never dreamed of anything so beautiful. They immediately believed that Alice must have prepared that sausage for their dinner. Extremely proud to have thought to bring the lentils, they settled in the wicker chairs to wait for Alice, who wouldn't be long.

They didn't move. Alice didn't come back.

Could they leave without talking to her? That was out of the question.

They fell asleep.

When the twins awoke, hunger was gnawing

dreadfully at them. Fulvio, being less timid, said aloud what Flavio had been thinking for quite a while.

"What about cooking some lentils and eating a bit of the sausage?"

"Without waiting for Alice?"

"You know her, she's so nice, she will be delighted to know we have eaten our fill."

Hearing those words, Alice opened the fatty slit which was now her eye. The twins, after so many months of absence, were standing next to her, whispering about how nice she was. Alice was on the verge of tears, her happiness seemed too copious. Finally her efforts were to be rewarded. She understood of course that the twins wanted to eat her. It didn't matter, she realized that her life would take on its whole meaning. In that desire for her, there was an absolute gratitude, a boundless trust. Those twins, whom she had sucked so often and so patiently, were going to devour her ... bit by bit. For the first time Alice felt an intense pleasure, close to ecstasy.

Fulvio and Flavio put the lentils on to cook,

took a little penknife they kept to slice the bread and *porchetta*, and started to cut the sausage.

Alice didn't scream. She was in pain but the moment was so exquisite, her happiness so intense. Here was the opportunity to be perfectly nice to the twins. The gift of herself finally took on its whole and entire meaning. She didn't utter a sound. At the third mouthful Alice passed out. It was never known if it was from pain or orgasm.

Fulvio and Flavio had a feast. Until that day they had eaten nothing so delicious. So mild. So well-flavoured. So unctuous. So tasty. By the end of that winter day, they had quietly relished the whole of Alice in a feast as unexpected as it was delicious.

Once the sausage and the lentils had been consumed they had a rest. Despairing of all hope of seeing their friend come back, they left her a note assuring her that the meal had been fantastic. They departed feeling light-hearted, promising to return soon to thank her.

When the twins came out into the street, the sky had cleared. There was one single cloud which looked down on them with affection as they passed. A cloud which wondered if the sausage meat had been unctuous enough, delicious enough, tender enough. The cloud smiled to see them so happy, but were they completely satisfied?

Even in heaven, Alice was trying to fathom out if she had been nice enough.

It was at that precise moment the parrot decided to speak. It had watched Alice's feast without opening its beak, but, moved by remorse, or regret, it finally let slip, between two bird sobs: "Alice the sausage, Alice the sausage."

It repeated those words till nightfall, without stopping, only ending when it dozed off on its perch, missing its owner and the seeds she used to dish out.

GLOSSARY OF ITALICIZED FOOD TERMS
IN THE TEXT

Cappuccino is, of course, a coffee with milk that some might like to drink in the morning.

Gorgonzola, mascarpone, mozzarella, provolone and *ricotta* are Italian cheeses.

Mortadella is a Bologna sausage made with pork or, in cheaper versions, a mixture of pork, veal, tripe, pig's head, perhaps donkey meat, along with other additives, all cooked by a steam process.

Salsiccia is a fresh link sausage often made from pork, to be cooked before eating.

Cannelloni, penne, pappardelle, and *lasagne* are different pasta shapes, namely: large-diameter tubes (that can be stuffed); stubby tubes with quill-shaped ends (i.e., cut diagonally); broad ribbons, often with crimped edges; and rectangular sheets.

Pasta alla carbonara is a pasta dish with ham or bacon and eggs.

Penne all'arrabbiata is a pasta dish with hot red chillis in a tomato sauce.

Gnocchi are little dumplings made of semolina flour, potato, or spinach and ricotta cheese, usually containing pieces of cheese and mortadella, cooked in boiling water and served with a sauce.

Pizza *napoletana* is the classic pizza with tomatoes, mozzarella, oregano and anchovies.

Pizza *bianca*, pizza *rossa*, and pizza *margherita* are, namely: plain with no topping (hence the name!); plain with tomato; and the last, named after Queen Margherita, is the colour of the national flag – white (mozzarella), red (tomato) and green (basil leaves).

Pizzette are miniature pizzas.

Calzone are half-moon shaped pizzette (folded in two, in other words), often stuffed with ham and cheese.

Prosciutto cotto is cooked ham.

Porchetta is roast sucking pig.

Bocconcini are little rolls of veal slices and ham stuffed with gruyère cheese, or morsels of fried ricotta balls, or veal stew, the Italian word referring to an appetizing 'mouthful'.

Calamaretti fritters are rings of squid fried in batter.

Aubergines *au gratin* are aubergines baked with a coating of grated parmesan cheese.

Suppli are rice croquettes with a centre of melted mozzarella and a piece of ham or mortadella or other fillings.

Grissini are little thin sticks of bread, originally made in Turin.

Rosette are bread rolls that resemble a flower.

Bruschetta are toasted slices of bread rubbed with garlic and covered in olive oil and served with various toppings of red pepper, tomato, cheese . . .

Tramezzini are sandwiches, often triangular-shaped, the word literally meaning 'in the middle', referring to the filling between the two slices of bread.

Ciambelle is a ring-shaped cake with a hollow centre.

Neapolitan *stracciatella is* vanilla ice cream with chocolate chips.

Baci Perugina, 'Perugia Kisses', are exquisite chocolates, hazelnuts in a praline 'enrobed' in a bittersweet chocolate.

(The Translators, with added thanks
to Christine Donougher)